Distance To Destiny

Mrigendra Bharti

Published by Sellbrochure Vymish Entertainment, 2024.

DISTANCE TO DESTINY

First edition. July 12, 2024.

ISBN: 979-8227918901

Written by Mrigendra Bharti.

Table of Contents

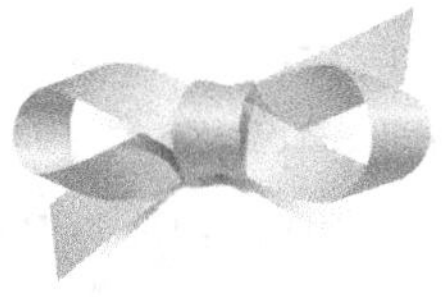

Preface

Love stories come in all shapes and sizes. Some bloom under the warm glow of familiarity, while others blossom amidst the challenges of distance. Ours, a vibrant tapestry woven with threads of art, science, and unwavering connection, defied convention. It's a story not just about love, but about the transformative power of collaboration, the resilience of the human spirit, and the enduring beauty that emerges when two souls find their perfect harmony.

This book is an invitation into our journey, a journey that began with a chance encounter and blossomed into a love story that transcended geographical boundaries. We were young, naive, and brimming with dreams – Anya, the aspiring scientist with a head full of theories and a heart yearning for exploration, and Kai, the passionate artist with a soul seeking expression and a canvas waiting to be filled.

Our paths collided in a bustling university laboratory, a spark igniting amidst the whirring centrifuges and bubbling beakers. Yet, even as our connection deepened, the realities of life threatened to pull us apart. Anya, captivated by research opportunities, found herself drawn to distant shores, while Kai, fueled by artistic aspirations, craved the energy of international exhibitions.

This book chronicles our struggles and triumphs as we grappled with the challenges of long-distance love. It explores the creative ways we nurtured our connection, using art and science as bridges to span the physical distance between us. You'll witness our tentative steps towards cohabitation, the joys and hurdles of merging our artistic temperaments, and the unwavering support we provided each other as we chased our individual dreams.

But most importantly, this book is a celebration of collaboration. It delves into the magic that unfolded when we combined our unique perspectives. Anya's scientific insights fueled Kai's artistic expressions, while Kai's creative spark ignited new avenues of exploration in Anya's research. Together, we discovered a world where art and science intersected, where data translated into stunning visuals, and scientific discoveries inspired artistic masterpieces.

Our journey wasn't always smooth sailing. There were moments of doubt, anxieties about careers, and the ever-present struggle to balance ambition with love. Yet, through it all, our commitment to each other remained unwavering. We learned to communicate openly, navigate the complexities of compromise, and find strength in each other's support.

This book is not just our story; it's an ode to the power of human connection. It's a testament to the enduring strength of love in the face of distance, a reminder that with trust, communication, and a willingness to adapt, even the most daunting challenges can be overcome. It's an invitation to embrace collaboration, to explore the beauty that arises when seemingly disparate worlds collide.

So, open this book and step into our world, a world where love paints vibrant strokes on the canvas of life, where science and art create a symphony for the soul, and where two hearts, intertwined by a love unlike any other, paint a masterpiece that continues to evolve with each passing day.

. . ❧ . .

WELCOME TO OUR STORY.

Prologue

In the sterile silence of a university research lab, amidst the whirring centrifuges and the clinking of glassware, a spark ignited. Anya, her brow furrowed in concentration as she meticulously examined a slide under the microscope, was oblivious to the symphony of scientific activity unfolding around her. Lost in the intricate dance of cells, she craved a deeper understanding, a way to bridge the gap between the microscopic world and the human experience.

Suddenly, a splash of vibrant color burst into her peripheral vision. Turning her head, she found herself face-to-face with Kai, a paintbrush dripping with azure blue, his eyes sparkling with a captivating mixture of mischief and artistic fervor. He was a whirlwind of creative energy, his presence a jarring yet oddly refreshing contrast to the sterile lab environment.

Their initial encounter was a collision of order and chaos, a scientist and an artist thrown together by happenstance. Yet, in that unexpected moment, an invisible thread of connection began to weave its way between them. It was a connection that defied definition, a spark of mutual curiosity that transcended the boundaries of their vastly different worlds.

This is not just a love story; it's a tale of resilience, of love blossoming amidst the challenges of distance, and of two individuals finding a shared language in the realms of art and science. It's a story painted on the canvas of life, each brushstroke a testament to their unwavering belief in the power of love and the transformative beauty of collaboration.

Prepare to be swept into a journey where scientific discoveries inspire artistic expressions, and where the distance between two hearts becomes a bridge built on communication, compromise, and an unwavering desire to create something extraordinary together. As we delve into the chapters that unfold, hold onto your curiosity, for you're about to witness the vibrant masterpiece that love painted in the colors of science and art.

About Sellbrochure Vymish Entertainment

Sellbrochure Vymish Entertainment, recognized as India's largest book publishing company, has made significant strides in ensuring its extensive collection of books reaches audiences across the global market. This rapid expansion is a testament to the company's dedication to disseminating knowledge and literature far beyond national borders. Central to its success is its affiliation with InkWhirl Media Networks, a reputable entity in the media and publication industry known for its innovative and strategic approaches. Within this network, InkWhirl Publication LLC operates as a vital division, further enhancing the company's capabilities and reach in the international market.

The visionary behind this enterprise is Mrigendra Bharti, the founder of Sellbrochure Vymish Entertainment. His foresight and passion for the literary world have been instrumental in steering the company towards remarkable growth and recognition. Under his leadership, Sellbrochure Vymish Entertainment has not only expanded its catalog but also established a strong presence in both domestic and international markets. Mrigendra Bharti's commitment to excellence and innovation has been a driving force in the company's journey, ensuring that it stays ahead of industry trends and meets the evolving needs of readers worldwide.

Sellbrochure Vymish Entertainment operates under the robust support of its parental organization, Mrigendra Bharti Group InfoTech. This affiliation provides the necessary resources and strategic guidance, enabling the publishing company to undertake ambitious projects and explore new markets. Mrigendra Bharti Group InfoTech's extensive experience in technology and information services has been a valuable asset, allowing Sellbrochure Vymish Entertainment to integrate advanced digital solutions in its operations, thereby enhancing its distribution capabilities and reader engagement.

Through relentless efforts and a commitment to quality, Sellbrochure Vymish Entertainment continues to break barriers and expand the reach of Indian literature globally. The company's diverse portfolio includes a wide range of genres, catering to different age groups and interests, thereby fostering a rich and inclusive reading culture. As it continues to innovate and grow, Sellbrochure Vymish Entertainment remains dedicated to its mission of making literature accessible to all, contributing significantly to the global literary landscape.

Connect With Mrigendra,
Thank you very much for choosing this book.
You can also connect with me on Instagram,
https://www.instagram.com/i_mrigendrabharti.official
With Love,
Mrigendra Bharti

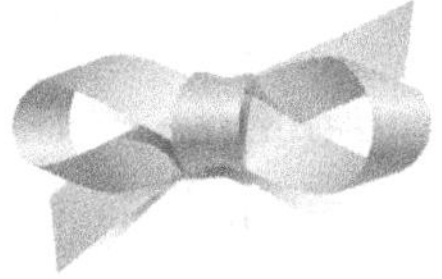

Introduction

Life rarely unfolds in a linear fashion. It's a messy, unpredictable journey, a canvas waiting to be splashed with the vibrant colors of experience. This book is an invitation to step into a story that defies convention, a love story woven with the threads of science, art, and an enduring connection.

We are Anya and Kai, and this is our tale. It all began in a bustling university laboratory, a place where the methodical pursuit of knowledge reigned supreme. Anya, a budding scientist with a mind brimming with theories and a heart yearning for exploration, found solace in the world of data and discovery. But amidst the sterile lab environment, a spark ignited, a vibrant counterpoint to the world of beakers and microscopes.

Enter Kai, an artist whose soul pulsed with creativity, his hands yearning to translate emotions onto canvas. He was a whirlwind of artistic energy, a splash of color in the world of scientific precision. Our paths collided unexpectedly, a scientist and an artist thrown together by chance. Yet, in that unexpected moment, a connection sparked, a shared curiosity that transcended the boundaries of our seemingly disparate worlds.

This book is a testament to the power of that connection, a love story that defied the challenges of distance. It chronicles our struggles and triumphs as we navigated the complexities of long-distance relationships, using art and science as bridges to span the physical divide. You'll witness our tentative steps towards cohabitation, the joys and hurdles of merging our artistic temperaments, and the unwavering support we provided each other as we chased our individual dreams.

But beyond the personal narrative, this book delves into the magic of collaboration. It explores the transformative power of uniting seemingly disparate disciplines, where data translates into stunning visuals, and scientific discoveries spark artistic masterpieces. We'll journey with you as we discover a world where art and science intersect, a world where creativity ignites new avenues of scientific exploration, and logic inspires artistic innovation.

Our story isn't just about love; it's a celebration of the human spirit, a testament to the enduring strength of connection in the face of distance. It's an invitation to embrace collaboration, to explore the beauty that arises when seemingly disparate worlds collide. Prepare to be swept into a journey where scientific discoveries inspire artistic expressions, and where communication, compromise, and unwavering love become the brushstrokes that paint a vibrant masterpiece on the canvas of life.

This is a story for anyone who has ever dared to dream beyond limitations, for anyone who believes in the transformative power of love, and for anyone who finds inspiration at the intersection of creativity and logic. So, turn the page and join us on this incredible adventure, where love paints vibrant strokes on the canvas of life, and science and art create a symphony for the soul.

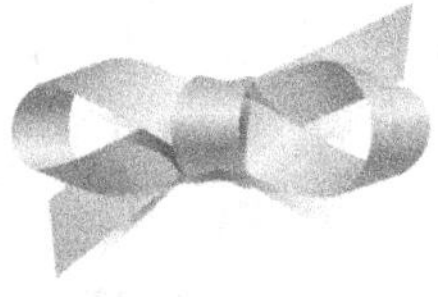

Chapter 1: The Spark

The scent of old textbooks and nervous perspiration hung heavy in the air of Westwood High's debate club room. Anya Sharma, a whirlwind of nervous energy, paced in front of the whiteboard, rehearsing her closing arguments. Her dark braid swished with each turn, the equations scrawled on the board testament to the intensity of her preparation. Tonight's topic – "Should artificial intelligence be granted legal rights?" – was a personal one for Anya. Raised in a Silicon Valley household where innovation was practically a religion, Anya believed AI held the potential to revolutionize humanity's progress.

Across the room, Kai Donovan sprawled languidly on a beanbag chair, his posture a stark contrast to Anya's tightly coiled tension. His gaze, however, was fixed on her, a spark of amusement dancing in his hazel eyes. Kai, the undisputed artist of their senior class, possessed a nonchalance that often masked a sharp intellect. He'd chosen the opposing side for the sheer entertainment of riling up Anya, their verbal sparring matches a highlight of the club's activities.

The moderator, Mr. Davis, a portly man with a perpetually surprised expression, rapped his gavel for silence. "Tonight, we have Anya Sharma arguing for the proposition and Kai Donovan arguing against it. Let the debate commence!"

Anya straightened her shoulders, her voice ringing with conviction as she launched into her opening statement. "Imagine a world where machines can think for themselves, solve complex problems, and even create art," she began, her voice gaining momentum with each word. "AI has the potential to alleviate human suffering, cure diseases, and propel us into a new era of progress. Denying them legal rights would be akin to denying a sentient being its basic rights."

Kai, unfazed by Anya's passionate delivery, rose from his beanbag with a lopsided grin. "Anya paints a beautiful picture, folks," he drawled, his voice laced with a hint of sarcasm. "But let's not forget that AI is a tool, a creation of human ingenuity. Granting them legal rights opens a Pandora's box of ethical dilemmas. What happens when an AI surpasses human intelligence and decides we're the ones who pose a threat?"

The audience, a mix of enthusiastic debaters and curious onlookers, murmured amongst themselves. Anya, stung by Kai's flippant tone, countered with a sharp retort. "Fear-mongering won't solve anything, Kai. We can establish safeguards, ethical guidelines to ensure responsible AI development. The potential benefits far outweigh the risks."

Their arguments flowed back and forth, a heated dance of logic and emotion. Anya, fueled by a deep-seated belief in the future of technology, marshaled facts and statistics. Kai, with his artist's eye for the unforeseen, weaved tales of dystopian futures controlled by rogue machines. The audience was enthralled, their initial amusement replaced by genuine investment in the clashing ideologies.

As the debate raged on, an undercurrent of something more than intellectual sparring crackled between Anya and Kai. Anya, usually laser-focused on her arguments, found herself stealing glances at Kai. His animated expressions, the way his unruly mop of brown hair flopped over his forehead with each emphatic point, sent a unfamiliar flutter in her chest. Kai, too, felt a strange shift in his attention. Anya's fiery passion, the glint of determination in her eyes, was far more captivating than any debate topic.

The back-and-forth banter continued, laced with subtle barbs that, to an outside observer, might have seemed playfully antagonistic. But Anya and Kai couldn't ignore the undercurrent of something else entirely. When Anya delivered a particularly scathing rebuttal, a ghost of a smile played on Kai's lips, his eyes twinkling with a challenge that sent a shiver down her spine. When Kai countered with a darkly humorous hypothetical scenario, Anya felt a warmth bloom in her cheeks, a reaction entirely unrelated to the debate itself.

The final bell signaling the end of the debate jerked them both back to reality. Anya, momentarily flustered by the shift in her own emotions, quickly launched into her closing arguments, her voice regaining its practiced composure. Kai, sensing her change, mirrored her seriousness, delivering a final thought-provoking question that left the audience pondering long after the gavel fell.

As the applause subsided, a comfortable silence descended upon the room. Anya, gathering her notes, met Kai's gaze across the room. The intensity in his eyes sent a jolt through her. He sauntered over, a hint of a smile playing on his lips.

"Well argued, Sharma," he said, extending a hand. "You almost had me convinced."

Anya, surprised by the compliment, took his hand. His touch lingered a beat too long, sending a spark up her arm.

"Don't get too cocky, Donovan," she countered, a playful glint in her eyes. "Your doomsday scenarios were entertaining, but hardly convincing."

Kai chuckled, a rich, melodic sound that sent shivers down her spine. "Perhaps we should take this debate outside the club room sometime," he suggested, his voice a low murmur. "Over coffee maybe? A neutral ground for a truce?"

Anya's heart skipped a beat. The idea of spending time with Kai outside of their usual debate battles was enticing, yet a flicker of uncertainty crossed her mind. Kai was different from her usual circle of friends, more carefree and unpredictable compared to her studious, ambitious nature.

Despite the reservations, Anya couldn't deny the strange pull she felt towards him. "Maybe," she replied, offering a noncommittal smile. "If I have the time between lectures and lab experiments."

Kai raised an eyebrow. "Busy schedule, I see. But hey, even geniuses need a break sometimes, right?"

Anya couldn't help but smile back. There was something about Kai's easy confidence that was disarming. As they walked out of the debate room together, a silent question hung in the air – was this the start of something more, or just another intellectual joust that had spilled over into their personal lives? Only time would tell.

Anya's life revolved around structure and predictability. Her days were meticulously planned, her evenings spent buried in textbooks or tinkering with complex algorithms in her home lab. Weekends were for catching up on lectures or attending science fairs, her mind constantly buzzing with ideas and theories.

Kai's world was a kaleidoscope of colors and emotions. He spent his days lost in his art studio, a converted garage overflowing with paint-splattered canvases and half-sculpted figures. His nights were filled with music, poetry readings, and impromptu gatherings with a motley crew of artists and musicians. Structure was anathema to him; he thrived on spontaneity and embraced the unexpected.

Despite their contrasting personalities, the connection sparked during their debate lingered. Anya found herself drawn to Kai's carefree spirit, his ability to see the world through a creative lens that challenged her own logical approach. Kai, in turn, was intrigued by Anya's sharp intellect and unwavering determination. He admired her passion for science, a field so different from his own artistic pursuits.

Anya hesitantly agreed to meet Kai for coffee after a particularly grueling week of exams. The cafe, a cozy little bookstore with the aroma of freshly brewed coffee and old paper, was a far cry from Anya's usual sterile study haunts. Kai, ever the charmer, managed to snag a table by the window, sunlight filtering through the leaves of a towering oak tree outside.

As they settled in, conversation flowed easily, albeit in fits and starts. Anya, still guarded by her natural shyness, spoke about her upcoming internship at a prestigious robotics lab. Kai, in turn, regaled her with tales of his latest art project, a series of sculptures that explored the concept of artificial intelligence.

Their conversation highlighted the vast differences in their worlds, yet an undercurrent of mutual respect kept them engaged. Anya was surprised by Kai's depth of knowledge about AI, his concerns about its potential impact surprisingly insightful. Kai, for his part, was captivated by Anya's passion for her work, the way her eyes lit up when she spoke about the possibilities of scientific discovery.

Despite their contrasting backgrounds, they discovered a surprising number of shared interests. They both loved classic science fiction, their discussions about the works of Asimov and Clarke filled with animated debate. They both held a deep-seated belief in the power of human potential, albeit expressed through different avenues.

As the afternoon wore on, a comfortable silence descended upon them. Anya found herself stealing glances at Kai, captivated by the way his brow furrowed in concentration as he sketched something on a napkin. Kai, catching her gaze, offered a lopsided grin, sending a blush creeping up Anya's cheeks.

The cafe's closing chime jolted them back to reality. As they stepped outside, the golden hues of the setting sun painted the sky in vibrant colors. Anya, for the first time in a long time, felt a sense of carefree joy, a lightness that defied her usual seriousness.

"This was..." Anya began, searching for the right words.

"Different?" Kai finished with a playful smile.

Anya nodded, a reluctant smile gracing her lips. "Different. In a good way."

The encounter left Anya with a newfound sense of curiosity. Kai's world, so different from her own, held a strange allure. And as they parted ways, a silent question lingered in the air – could their connection bridge the gap between their contrasting worlds, or was it destined to remain a fleeting moment of shared understanding?

The days that followed Anya's coffee date with Kai were filled with a strange sense of anticipation. Stolen glances across the debate room, lingering touches during group projects, and late-night text messages discussing everything from astrophysics to their favorite childhood cartoons – a tentative friendship began to blossom between them.

Anya, initially hesitant to step outside her comfort zone, found herself drawn into Kai's world. She accompanied him to a gallery opening, her initial skepticism melting away as she witnessed the raw emotion poured into the artwork. Kai, in turn, surprised her by attending her science fair presentation, his questions about her robotic project thoughtful and insightful.

Their newfound friendship wasn't without its challenges. Anya's friends, a studious bunch laser-focused on college applications, viewed Kai with suspicion. His artistic pursuits and carefree demeanor clashed with their more conventional ambitions. Kai's circle, a motley crew of free spirits, found Anya's intensity and structured life somewhat intimidating.

Despite the whispers and raised eyebrows, Anya and Kai persevered. They carved out stolen moments for each other, their connection deepening with each shared experience. Anya found herself confiding in Kai about her anxieties about the upcoming internship, his unwavering belief in her abilities a source of unexpected comfort. Kai, struggling with a creative block, found inspiration in Anya's logical approach, her ability to break down complex ideas sparking a renewed sense of purpose in his art.

One crisp autumn afternoon, they found themselves exploring a secluded hiking trail, a kaleidoscope of vibrant colors beneath their feet. As they reached a scenic overlook, Kai surprised Anya by pulling out a worn sketchbook and a box of charcoal pencils.

"I wanted to capture this," he said, gesturing at the breathtaking vista before them. "But your perspective might be helpful."

Anya, flattered by his request, settled beside him. They spent the next hour lost in conversation, Kai sketching the landscape while Anya pointed out the intricate details – the way the sunlight danced on the leaves, the geological formations of the rocks beneath their feet.

As the sun began its descent, casting long shadows across the valley, Kai turned to Anya, a hint of shyness in his eyes. "This is nice," he admitted, his voice barely a whisper. "Spending time with you, outside of debates and science fairs."

Anya felt her cheeks flush. "It's nice for me too," she replied softly.

The unspoken sentiment hung heavy in the air. Anya, for the first time, acknowledged the growing feelings for Kai that had blossomed beneath the surface. Kai, too, felt a shift in their connection, a yearning for something more than just friendship.

The hike back was filled with a comfortable silence, a silent understanding passing between them. As they reached the trailhead, Kai stopped abruptly, his gaze fixed on Anya.

"There's something I want to ask you," he began, his voice hesitant.

Anya's heart pounded in her chest. Could this be the start of something more? As Kai leaned in, his question hanging in the air, the chapter ends, leaving the reader eager to discover the next step in Anya and Kai's evolving relationship.

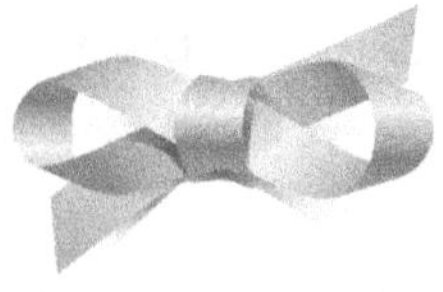

Chapter 2: Love's Long Journey

The acceptance letter from Stanford, Anya's dream school, arrived on a crisp spring morning, bursting with the promise of a bright future. Anya, usually stoic and composed, squealed with delight, the culmination of years of relentless hard work finally within reach. Yet, amidst the celebratory phone calls and congratulatory messages, a knot of worry tightened in her stomach.

Stanford was across the country, a daunting distance that threatened to disrupt the connection she'd forged with Kai. Their friendship, once a tentative spark, had blossomed into a full-fledged romance. Stolen glances in the hallways had morphed into whispered secrets under the cloak of twilight, their bond deepening with every shared experience.

Kai, ever the artist, had captured Anya's essence in a charcoal portrait – her fiery spirit and unwavering determination etched in the intensity of her gaze. Anya, in turn, had surprised Kai with a custom-designed algorithm that generated color palettes based on his emotions, a testament to her love and her ingenuity.

The prospect of leaving Kai behind cast a shadow on Anya's excitement. They spent their evenings huddled together, poring over maps and calculating time differences. Anya, the ever-practical one, explored possibilities for long-distance relationships, bombarding Kai with research articles and statistics on successful couples navigating geographical separation.

Kai, more apprehensive about the unknown, listened patiently, a hint of worry clouding his usual carefree demeanor. He wasn't one for grand gestures or sentimental pronouncements, but his love for Anya shone through in the quiet moments – the way his hand lingered on hers a beat too long, the comfortable silence that enveloped them as they sat together, lost in their own world.

As the weight of reality settled in, Anya and Kai grappled with the impending distance. Anya, a planner by nature, dove headfirst into research, scouring the internet for tips on surviving long-distance relationships. She compiled meticulous schedules, color-coded spreadsheets outlining communication plans, determined to maintain the closeness they'd built.

Kai, on the other hand, struggled with the idea of expressing his emotions through phone calls and video chats. He preferred the intimacy of shared experiences, the comfort of stolen glances and whispered secrets that transcended words. The prospect of their connection being reduced to pixelated images on a screen filled him with a quiet despair.

Their contrasting approaches led to their first significant argument. Anya, frustrated by Kai's seeming lack of enthusiasm for her meticulously crafted communication plan, accused him of not being invested in their future. Kai, stung by her words, retreated into his usual shell, his silence a stark contrast to Anya's emotional outburst.

The following days were strained. Anya, consumed by guilt, apologized for her outburst, but a sense of uncertainty lingered. Kai, still grappling with his anxieties, offered a tentative suggestion – a promise to visit Anya at Stanford during every semester break.

Anya, touched by his gesture, readily agreed. It wasn't the perfectly regimented plan she'd envisioned, but it offered a beacon of hope, a chance to bridge the physical gap with cherished moments together. As they tentatively reconciled, a newfound understanding bloomed between them. They realized that love, like their personalities, wouldn't be confined to neat categories or color-coded schedules. It would require flexibility, compromise, and a deep-seated faith in the strength of their connection.

Stanford beckoned with a whirlwind of academic rigor and exhilarating new experiences. Anya, initially overwhelmed by the pressure and unfamiliar social circles, found solace in the comfort of late-night video calls with Kai. They'd share stories of their days, Kai regaling her with tales of his latest art project, Anya excitedly describing her groundbreaking research on biomimetic robotics. Despite the physical distance, these virtual conversations kept them connected, a lifeline amidst the challenges of their new realities.

However, the idyllic image Anya had envisioned of their long-distance relationship began to crack. Time zones became a constant hurdle, stolen moments snatched between Anya's jam-packed schedule and Kai's late-night artistic endeavors. The pixelated faces on the screen couldn't quite capture the warmth of a shared embrace or the comfort of a hand resting in hers.

The physical separation fueled anxieties. Anya, bombarded with new social interactions and academic pressures, began to question Kai's place in her life. Was their connection strong enough to withstand the miles and the ever-growing distance between their experiences? Kai, grappling with feelings of inadequacy amidst Anya's blossoming academic success, felt a pang of insecurity. Was his artistic life, filled with uncertainty and financial struggles, a poor match for Anya's bright future on the scientific stage?

These unspoken doubts manifested in clipped conversations and strained silences during their video calls. Anya, stressed and sleep-deprived, misinterpreted Kai's quiet support as a lack of interest. Kai, misconstruing Anya's laser focus on her studies as a sign of emotional detachment, retreated further into his shell.

A particularly tense call ended with a frustrated Anya slamming her laptop shut, tears welling up in her eyes. The distance, once a manageable hurdle, now felt like an insurmountable chasm, threatening to swallow their connection whole. As the days turned into weeks, the once vibrant thread of communication began to fray, leaving them both feeling adrift and alone.

The silence stretched on for weeks, a heavy weight pressing down on Anya and Kai. Anya, consumed by guilt and a gnawing sense of loss, threw herself into her studies with renewed fervor. The once-thrilling world of scientific discovery now felt like a hollow pursuit, devoid of the joy it once held. Kai, his studio a testament to his creative ennui, found himself lost in a sea of unfinished paintings and discarded sculptures. The vibrant colors that once flowed from his brush seemed muted, reflecting the dull ache of their fractured connection.

One evening, amidst the deafening silence of her dorm room, Anya stumbled upon a forgotten box tucked away in her closet. Inside, nestled amongst childhood keepsakes and old photographs, lay the charcoal portrait Kai had gifted her. As she traced the familiar lines of her face captured in his art, a wave of emotions washed over her – love, regret, and a fierce determination to win him back.

Fueled by a newfound resolve, Anya reached out to Kai, not through a scheduled video call, but with a handwritten letter. Pouring her heart onto the page, she confessed her anxieties, her insecurities, and the depth of her love for him. She acknowledged the challenges of their long-distance relationship but emphasized her unwavering belief in their connection.

Days turned into weeks with no response from Kai. The silence gnawed at Anya, each passing day amplifying her fear that their love story had reached its final chapter. Just as despair threatened to consume her, a worn envelope arrived in the mail, the familiar scrawl on the front sending a jolt of hope through her.

Kai's reply was a heartfelt outpouring of his emotions. He confessed his own insecurities, his fear of not being enough for her ever-evolving world. But his love for Anya shone through his words, a beacon of hope in the darkness of their separation. He proposed a solution – a compromise born out of their unique circumstances.

Instead of rigid schedules and forced conversations, they would embrace the spontaneity of their connection. Letters, care packages filled with tokens of their love, surprise phone calls at odd hours – these would become the new threads weaving the tapestry of their relationship. They would focus on cherishing the moments they had, both virtual and during Kai's promised visits, nurturing their love amidst the miles that separated them.

Anya, a flicker of hope rekindled in her eyes, wrote back immediately, her reply echoing Kai's sentiments. They wouldn't let the distance define them. Their love, unconventional and ever-evolving, would find a way to bridge the gap, stronger and more resilient for having weathered the storm.

As they reconnected, their communication flowed with a newfound honesty. They embraced the flexibility of their long-distance dynamic, the surprise letters and late-night calls becoming cherished moments in their evolving relationship.

Anya learned to appreciate the depth of Kai's love expressed through his art, a silent language that transcended the limitations of video calls. Kai, inspired by Anya's resilience, found his artistic voice again, his paintings infused with a newfound vibrancy that mirrored their rekindled connection.

Theirs was a love story that defied convention, a testament to the enduring power of connection that could bridge geographical distances and navigate the complexities of life. As Anya awaited Kai's first visit to Stanford, a nervous excitement thrummed beneath her surface. The miles that separated them might not disappear, but their love, strengthened by the challenges they'd faced, had grown into something extraordinary, a beacon guiding them towards a future they would build together.

Chapter 3: Misunderstandings and Heartbreak

Summer break arrived, a welcome respite from the relentless pace of Stanford. Anya, eager to reconnect with Kai face-to-face, meticulously planned their visit. Days were filled with exploring hidden cafes, visiting quirky art galleries, and simply reveling in each other's company. Evenings were spent under the starlit sky, sharing dreams and anxieties, their laughter echoing through the quiet nights.

Kai, basking in Anya's radiant presence, felt a surge of inspiration. He rented a small cabin nestled amidst a secluded redwood forest, a haven for him to express his artistic vision. Anya, ever supportive, encouraged him to focus on his art, offering to handle errands and chores to give him uninterrupted creative time.

The initial bliss, however, was short-lived. Anya, accustomed to the structured routine of her academic life, found herself restless amidst the unstructured days at the cabin. The silence, once a canvas for their conversations, now stretched uncomfortably between them. Kai, consumed by his creative fervor, became oblivious to Anya's growing unease.

One evening, as the remnants of a magnificent sunset painted the sky in fiery hues, Anya hesitantly approached Kai, who was hunched over his latest canvas. "It's beautiful," she said softly, her voice barely a whisper.

Kai, startled from his concentration, looked up with a smile. "Thanks," he replied, his gaze lingering on her face for a beat too long. "What's on your mind?"

Anya fidgeted with the hem of her shirt, struggling to voice her concerns. "It just feels...different," she began cautiously. "The silence. I miss our talks, our debates about everything and nothing."

Kai frowned, a flicker of annoyance crossing his features. "We can talk later," he said dismissively, his attention already drifting back to his painting.

Anya felt a pang of hurt. "But Kai," she persisted, her voice trembling slightly, "I miss feeling connected. Like we're on the same page, you know?"

Kai sighed, his frustration evident. "Anya, I'm trying to create here. Can't you see that requires focus?"

His words stung. Anya, hurt by his dismissive tone, retreated to a corner of the cabin, a knot of frustration tightening in her stomach. The idyllic summer visit she'd envisioned was unraveling, replaced by a sense of growing distance.

Days turned into a tense silence. Anya, feeling unheard and neglected, busied herself with long walks in the woods, the solitude a balm to her wounded spirit. Kai, oblivious to the depth of her hurt, remained engrossed in his art, his creative energy seemingly at an all-time high.

One rainy afternoon, while rummaging through an old bookstore in a nearby town, Anya stumbled upon a dusty self-help book titled "Bridging the Gap: Communication Strategies for Long-Distance Couples." The title seemed a cruel joke, a stark reminder of the chasm that seemed to be widening between her and Kai. Yet, desperate for answers, she bought the book, a flicker of hope battling against the growing despair in her heart.

The self-help book offered a glimmer of hope amidst the growing storm in Anya and Kai's relationship. It spoke of the importance of open communication, active listening, and celebrating each other's individuality. Anya devoured the book, highlighting passages and making notes in the margins, a desperate attempt to salvage the connection she felt slipping away.

As the rain continued its relentless drumming against the cabin roof, Anya steeled herself for a conversation with Kai. She found him in his makeshift studio, surrounded by half-finished paintings and overflowing ashtrays. The air hung heavy with the acrid scent of cigarettes and the tension that had been simmering between them.

"Kai, we need to talk," Anya announced, her voice firm despite the tremor in her heart.

Kai looked up, his expression a mixture of surprise and apprehension. He set down his paintbrush, a silent invitation for her to proceed.

Anya took a deep breath, her gaze fixed on the swirling patterns on the wooden floor. "This isn't working," she began, her voice barely above a whisper. "The distance, the lack of communication... it's driving a wedge between us."

Kai remained silent, his jaw clenched, his eyes reflecting a storm of emotions.

"I miss the way we used to be," Anya continued, tears welling up in her eyes. "The way we could talk for hours about anything and everything. Now, it feels like we're living in separate worlds."

Anya's words hung heavy in the air. Kai finally broke the silence, his voice low and laced with frustration. "You don't understand, Anya. This is important to me. My art, my passion."

"And what about me?" Anya countered, her voice rising a notch. "What about our relationship? Does that not matter anymore?"

The conversation spiraled into a heated exchange, a torrent of unspoken hurt and frustration overflowing. Anya accused Kai of being selfish, of prioritizing his art over their connection. Kai, feeling misunderstood and unappreciated, lashed out, questioning her commitment to their unconventional relationship.

As the argument reached its crescendo, a deafening silence descended upon the cabin. The rain outside had stopped, but the storm within them raged on. Anya, tears streaming down her face, stormed out of the cabin, seeking solace in the cool night air. Kai, his head buried in his hands, slumped onto a nearby chair, the weight of their fight settling upon him like a leaden cloak.

The night stretched on, a cold emptiness replacing the warmth that had once filled the cabin. Anya, huddled beneath a towering oak tree, replayed the argument in her mind, each harsh word echoing in the stillness. Kai, staring blankly at his unfinished paintings, felt a crushing sense of despair. The future they had once envisioned, a future built on love and understanding, seemed to crumble before his very eyes.

The following morning dawned, a stark contrast to the turmoil of the previous night. A cold, clear light filtered through the trees, casting long shadows across the clearing. Anya emerged from her makeshift shelter under the oak tree, her face pale and drawn, her eyes red-rimmed from tears. The fight with Kai hung heavy in the air, a bitter taste lingering on her tongue.

Kai, his usually messy hair disheveled and dark circles etched beneath his eyes, sat hunched over, staring at the canvas untouched since their argument. The room, once bustling with his artistic energy, now felt devoid of life, a reflection of the despair that gnawed at him.

Anya, despite the hurt that pulsed within her, knew they couldn't avoid talking. Taking a deep breath, she approached Kai, her voice laced with a hint of trepidation.

"Kai," she began, "we can't just bury our heads in the sand. We need to talk, to understand each other."

Kai reluctantly lifted his head, his gaze meeting hers for the first time since their fight. He looked weary, defeated. "What's the point, Anya?" he croaked, his voice hoarse. "Maybe we just... don't work."

The words struck Anya like a physical blow. The very foundation of their relationship, the belief that they could overcome any obstacle, seemed to crumble. Yet, a flicker of hope remained.

"Maybe not," Anya countered, her voice gaining strength, "but we won't know unless we try. Can we at least attempt to bridge this gap?"

Kai remained silent for a long moment, his brow furrowed in contemplation. Finally, he sighed, a hint of resignation in his voice. "Alright," he conceded. "Let's talk."

The conversation that unfolded wasn't easy. It was a raw, honest exchange of emotions, filled with apologies, admissions of fault, and a desperate attempt to understand each other's perspectives. Anya confessed her struggles with the lack of communication, feeling like an outsider in the world Kai had created for himself. Kai, in turn, expressed his anxieties about his artistic pursuits, fearing that his passion wouldn't be enough for Anya's ambitious future.

As they spoke, a fragile understanding began to form. They realized their mistake – the assumption that their love could bridge any distance without deliberate effort. They acknowledged the unique challenges of their long-distance relationship, the need for more open communication, and a willingness to compromise.

The conversation didn't offer any easy answers. It left them with a bittersweet reality – their love wouldn't magically erase the distance or their differing personalities. But it did provide them with a crucial piece – a shared commitment to fight for their connection, to nurture their love even when miles separated them.

The remaining days of Anya's visit were imbued with a newfound sense of purpose. They explored artistic expressions from different cultures, finding common ground in the beauty and diversity of human creativity. Anya offered constructive criticism on Kai's art, highlighting its strengths while gently suggesting areas for improvement. Kai, reciprocating the gesture, encouraged Anya's creative side, suggesting she explore sketching as a way to unwind from her academic stress.

The day of Anya's departure arrived, a poignant reminder of the cruel distance that separated them. As they stood at the cabin doorway, a heavy silence enveloped them.

"I don't want to leave," Anya confessed, her voice choked with emotion.

Kai reached out, pulling her into a tight embrace. "Neither do I," he replied, his voice rough with unspoken emotions.

As they pulled apart, Kai held her gaze, his eyes filled with a newfound determination. "This isn't the end, Anya," he promised. "We'll figure this out, together."

Anya offered a wavering smile, a flicker of hope igniting in her eyes. "Together," she echoed, her voice barely a whisper.

Their goodbye was a silent plea, a promise to bridge the distance, not just with physical visits but with unwavering love and open communication. As Anya drove away, a single tear rolled down her cheek. The future remained uncertain, but they had each other, a connection they were determined to nurture, no matter the miles that separated them.

The weeks that followed Anya's departure were a test of their newfound resolve. Back at Stanford, Anya threw herself back into her studies, the familiar routine providing a semblance of comfort. Yet, the silence from Kai gnawed at her. The self-help book, once a beacon of hope, now lay forgotten on her nightstand, its promises feeling hollow in the face of their uncertain future.

Kai, on the other hand, found himself paralyzed by a creative block. The once vibrant colors on his canvas seemed muted, a reflection of the emptiness that had settled in the cabin after Anya's departure. The silence, once a canvas for his creativity, now echoed with the ghost of their argument, a constant reminder of the challenges that lay ahead.

One evening, as the California sun dipped below the horizon, casting long shadows across Anya's dorm room, a notification on her phone startled her. It was a message from Kai, not a text filled with words, but a picture. It depicted a breathtaking landscape, a vista of rolling hills bathed in the golden hues of sunset, with a single line accompanying it: "Thinking of you."

Anya's heart leaped. It was a simple gesture, yet it spoke volumes. It was a reminder that despite the distance, they were still connected, their hearts tethered by an invisible thread. She quickly replied with a picture of the Stanford campus bathed in the soft glow of moonlight, her own message short but filled with unspoken emotion: "Me too."

From that day on, a new form of communication blossomed between them. Pictures, short video clips, and voice notes became their language of love, a way to share snippets of their lives, their joys and frustrations, across the miles. Anya documented her scientific breakthroughs, her messages filled with an infectious excitement. Kai shared his artistic journey, his voice notes filled with a renewed passion as he described the inspiration behind his latest pieces.

The distance remained, a constant hurdle, but their communication, once strained, evolved into a rich tapestry woven with shared experiences and unspoken affection. They scheduled regular video calls, not rigid, pre-planned events, but spontaneous bursts of connection, fueled by a genuine desire to see and hear each other.

Their commitment to understanding each other's worlds grew stronger. Anya started attending art exhibits on campus, her appreciation for Kai's passion deepening with every brushstroke she witnessed. Kai, in turn, devoured articles about Anya's research, his admiration for her dedication burning ever brighter.

The challenges didn't disappear entirely. Time zone differences remained a constant source of frustration. There were moments of loneliness, pangs of longing for a shared embrace under the starlit sky. But through it all, their love persevered. They learned to celebrate the joys of their individual lives, knowing that they shared those experiences, in spirit, with each other.

As the months rolled by, a sense of purpose bloomed within their relationship. They began brainstorming ways to bridge the physical gap. Anya, inspired by Kai's artistic vision, proposed a collaborative project – a series of paintings depicting the beauty of science, each piece accompanied by a scientific explanation written by Anya. Kai, captivated by the idea, readily agreed.

Their project became a symbol of their love story – a testament to the power of their connection, a bridge that transcended geographical boundaries. It was a work of art that celebrated their unique strengths, their individual passions woven together into a stunning tapestry of love and understanding.

As they finalized their project, a sense of accomplishment washed over them. It was a reminder that despite the miles, they were a team, two halves of a whole, forever connected by the invisible thread of love. The future remained uncertain, but they faced it together, their love story a testament to the enduring power of connection, a beacon guiding them towards a future they would build, brick by brick, across the miles that separated them.

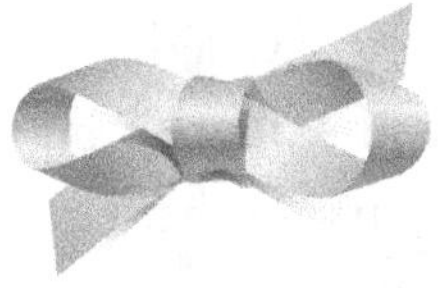

Chapter 4: A New Horizon

The crisp autumn air swirled with fallen leaves as Anya disembarked from the plane, a familiar mix of excitement and apprehension tingling in her stomach. After a year of navigating their long-distance relationship, she was finally returning to Kai's hometown for a three-month internship at a prestigious research facility. It was a chance to bridge the physical gap for an extended period, a test of their commitment and a step towards a future they were slowly building together.

Kai, waiting patiently at the arrivals gate, his face etched with a nervous smile, was the first person Anya saw. Relief washed over her as she rushed into his arms, the familiar warmth of his embrace a comforting balm after months of longing. The following weeks were a whirlwind of settling in, exploring the quaint town with its cobbled streets and cozy cafes, and most importantly, rediscovering the simple joy of spending time with Kai, hand-in-hand.

Anya's internship at the research facility proved to be both challenging and rewarding. She found herself collaborating with a team of passionate scientists, their shared thirst for knowledge creating a stimulating and supportive environment. Despite the long hours spent in the lab, her evenings were filled with laughter and shared dreams as she and Kai explored local art galleries and hidden trails, their relationship blossoming with each passing day.

The project they had initiated – a series of paintings depicting the beauty of science – continued to evolve. Anya, after a long day at the lab, would excitedly share her discoveries with Kai, her technical explanations sparking his artistic imagination. Kai, in turn, would translate his newfound scientific understanding into vibrant colors and captivating textures on his canvas.

However, their newfound bliss wasn't without its challenges. Anya, accustomed to the structured routines of Stanford, found herself overwhelmed by the unpredictability of Kai's artistic life. His late nights at the studio, fueled by bursts of creative inspiration, clashed with her meticulous schedule, leading to occasional arguments about priorities and stolen hours of sleep.

Kai, on the other hand, grappled with feelings of inadequacy amidst Anya's burgeoning scientific career. Surrounded by her brilliant colleagues and cutting-edge research, he questioned whether his artistic pursuits were enough, a nagging insecurity gnawing at his self-confidence.

These challenges, though seemingly insurmountable at times, became opportunities for growth. They learned to compromise, to find a balance between their individual passions and their shared goals. Anya, acknowledging the importance of Kai's artistic freedom, made a conscious effort to be more understanding of his late nights. Kai, inspired by Anya's dedication, started incorporating more discipline into his creative process, ensuring he dedicated quality time to both his art and their relationship.

As the weeks turned into months, a deeper understanding blossomed between Anya and Kai. They discovered a newfound appreciation for each other's worlds. Anya, initially dismissive of Kai's artistic struggles, found herself captivated by the emotional rawness and vulnerability he poured onto his canvas. She began to see art not just as a form of expression but as a window into the complexities of human experience.

Kai, in turn, developed a newfound fascination with Anya's scientific pursuits. He accompanied her to lab tours, his eyes gleaming with curiosity as she explained the intricacies of her research. The more he learned about the scientific world, the more he saw its connection to his own artistic vision – a shared language of observation, interpretation, and creation.

Their shared project became a symbol of their evolving relationship. As they collaborated, their individual strengths intertwined, creating a synergy far greater than the sum of its parts. Anya's scientific knowledge gave birth to captivating themes for Kai's paintings, while his artistic interpretation offered a unique perspective on complex scientific concepts.

One evening, as they stood in a local gallery, their collaborative artwork on display for the first time, a sense of accomplishment welled up within them. The vibrant colors and meticulously detailed explanations resonated with the audience, sparking conversations about the intersection of science and art. More importantly, it was a testament to their enduring love, a love that thrived on understanding and mutual respect.

However, the looming end of Anya's internship cast a shadow of uncertainty on their newfound happiness. The thought of returning to Stanford, of being miles apart once again, filled them with a familiar pang of longing. One starlit night, as they sat on a park bench overlooking the twinkling cityscape, Anya confessed her anxieties.

"What happens when I leave?" she asked, her voice laced with apprehension. "Can we make this work, long distance again?"

Kai took her hand, his gaze unwavering. "We've faced challenges before, Anya," he replied gently. "And together, we've grown stronger. We'll find a way."

His words offered a flicker of hope, a testament to their commitment. They spent the remaining weeks cherishing every moment, forging memories they could hold onto during the inevitable separation. They explored hidden waterfalls, hand-in-hand, the roar of the water a metaphor for the wild intensity of their love. They shared stolen kisses under starlit skies, whispering promises of a future they would build together.

The day of Anya's departure arrived, a poignant reminder of the cruel distance that separated them. As they embraced at the airport, tears streamed down Anya's face. This time, however, the tears weren't just of sadness, but of the bittersweet realization that their love story, though tested by miles, had only grown stronger.

As Anya settled back into her life at Stanford, a wave of loneliness washed over her. The comfort of Kai's presence, the warmth of his embrace, felt like a distant memory. Yet, amidst the ache of separation, a newfound resolve took root. They had weathered storms before, and they would weather this one too.

Their communication remained a vital lifeline. Late-night video calls, filled with laughter and shared stories, became a cherished ritual. Anya filled him in on her academic pursuits, her voice filled with an infectious enthusiasm. Kai, in turn, shared his artistic journey, his voice brimming with newfound confidence.

This time, however, their long-distance connection was fueled by a shared purpose – a plan for the future. Anya, inspired by their collaborative project, began exploring research opportunities that intersected science and art. Kai, empowered by Anya's belief in his talent, started working on a solo exhibition, showcasing his unique blend of scientific inspiration and artistic expression.

The miles that separated them only served to strengthen their resolve. They were two parts of a whole, their individual journeys converging towards a future they were building together, brick by brick, across the vast expanse of distance. Theirs was a love story that defied convention, a testament to the enduring power of connection, a beacon guiding them towards a future they would etch together, a masterpiece painted on the grand canvas of life.

Months flew by in a whirlwind of activity, fueled by a shared purpose. Anya, brimming with excitement, landed a research position at a prestigious institute dedicated to the intersection of art and science. It was the perfect opportunity to delve deeper into a field that had blossomed from their collaboration with Kai.

Meanwhile, Kai's solo exhibition, aptly titled "Chromatic Symphony," garnered widespread acclaim. His paintings, infused with both scientific themes and artistic expression, captivated audiences with their originality and depth. Anya, watching a live stream of the opening night from her dorm room, felt a surge of pride. Kai, his eyes searching for her amidst the crowd, found her face on the screen, their connection transcending the miles.

Their long-distance communication evolved into a creative collaboration once again. Anya, inspired by a new scientific discovery, sent Kai detailed descriptions of the phenomenon, its intricate beauty resonating with her scientific mind. Kai, in turn, used her descriptions as a springboard, translating them into stunning visuals, a symphony of colors and textures capturing the essence of Anya's research.

This newfound synergy wasn't limited to their professional lives. Their late-night video calls became more than just updates and shared stories. They discussed their artistic visions, bouncing ideas off each other, their individual perspectives enriching the other's creative process. Anya, once hesitant to explore her own artistic side, found herself sketching alongside Kai, his encouragement sparking a hidden passion.

As the months progressed, the question of their future loomed large. Anya, deeply invested in her research, knew she couldn't ignore the incredible opportunity she had been given. Kai, on the cusp of artistic recognition, couldn't walk away from the momentum he had built. Yet, the thought of enduring another long-distance separation filled them with dread.

One particularly emotional video call, as they lay in their separate beds, the silence pressing down on them, Anya broke down. "I don't want to be apart anymore, Kai," she confessed, her voice choked with tears.

Kai, mirroring her emotions, his voice raspy from unspoken longing, replied, "Neither do I, Anya. But what can we do?"

A thoughtful silence descended upon them. Then, Anya, her eyes sparkling with a newfound determination, spoke up. "What if we...tried something different?"

Intrigued, Kai raised an eyebrow, a flicker of hope igniting in his eyes. "Different?"

Anya took a deep breath. "What if we explored the possibility of living together? Maybe not permanently, but for a trial period. You could find a studio space here, I could continue my research, and we could finally be in the same place."

Kai's initial hesitation melted away as he considered the proposal. The thought of sharing a life, not just conversations across a screen, filled him with an unbridled joy. "Anya," he began, his voice thick with emotion, "That's... that's brilliant."

Anya's smile, brighter than the starlit night sky visible through her window, mirrored his excitement. They spent the next few hours meticulously planning, fueled by the prospect of a future together. It wouldn't be easy, there would be logistical hurdles and compromises to be made, but they were determined to make it work.

The following weeks were a flurry of activity. Anya contacted her department head, explaining her desire to explore a cohabitation arrangement with an artist-in-residence program in mind. Kai, buoyed by the prospect of being with Anya, negotiated a temporary studio space near the university, a place where his art could flourish alongside their shared life.

The day Anya arrived at their new apartment, a modest but cozy space filled with the promise of shared dreams, Kai greeted her at the door, a bouquet of sunflowers – Anya's favorite – in his arms. As they embraced, the weight of the distance they had endured lifted, replaced by the exhilarating feeling of finally being together.

Their journey had been long and arduous, filled with misunderstandings, heartache, and the ever-present challenge of physical separation. Yet, their love, nurtured by communication, compromise, and a shared commitment, had only grown stronger. They had learned to bridge the distance not just with words and technology, but with a deep understanding and unwavering belief in their connection.

As Anya stepped into their new home, hand in hand with Kai, their love story wasn't ending, it was just beginning. It was a story painted in vibrant colors, a testament to the enduring power of love, a love that had defied convention and had finally found its canvas – a life shared, a future built together.

Living together wasn't a fairytale. There were adjustments to be made, compromises to be navigated. Anya's early mornings for lab work clashed with Kai's late-night bursts of artistic inspiration. Shared living space meant learning to navigate each other's creative clutter and respecting individual routines.

Yet, the joys far outweighed the challenges. Stepping out the door in the morning and seeing Kai across the breakfast table, his sleep-tousled hair framing a smile brighter than the morning sun, was a constant reminder of the fight they had won. Weekend mornings were spent exploring farmers markets, their laughter echoing through the aisles as they picked out fresh ingredients for a shared brunch – a messy, joyful affair that solidified their sense of togetherness.

Their cohabitation arrangement became a source of inspiration for their work. Anya, witnessing Kai's struggle to balance artistic freedom with financial realities, began exploring grant opportunities that could support artists like him. Kai, in turn, incorporated her research findings into his latest series, creating stunning visuals that brought complex scientific concepts to life in a way that resonated with a wider audience.

Their apartment became a vibrant hub of creativity. Anya's meticulously organized workspace existed in comfortable chaos alongside Kai's paint-splattered haven. Late nights weren't just for video calls anymore, but for stolen moments of shared inspiration. Anya would sketch anatomical structures while Kai experimented with color palettes, their quiet companionship fueling their individual artistic journeys.

One evening, as they sat on their shared balcony, the city lights twinkling below like scattered stars, Anya turned to Kai, a question lingering in her eyes. "Do you think we can make this work, permanently?"

Kai, his gaze fixed on the cityscape, a smile playing on his lips, replied, "We already have, Anya. We just needed to find the right canvas."

Anya's heart swelled with joy. Their journey had been a rollercoaster, a testament to the enduring power of love despite the miles that had separated them. They had faced challenges head-on, emerging stronger with a deeper understanding of each other and their individual needs.

Their story wasn't over. There would be new obstacles, new hurdles to overcome. The future remained an open canvas, waiting to be painted with the vibrant colors of their love, their shared dreams, and their unwavering commitment to one another. But one thing was certain – they would face it together, hand in hand, a testament to the enduring power of love that had defied distance and blossomed into a masterpiece of their own making.

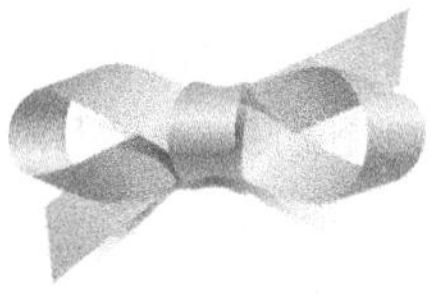

Chapter 5: The Colors of Change

Five years had passed since Anya and Kai had embarked on their cohabitation experiment. Their modest apartment, once a canvas of new beginnings, now held the comfortable patina of shared memories. The once-cluttered space had evolved into a harmonious blend of Anya's organized efficiency and Kai's artistic whimsy, a reflection of their intertwined lives.

Their careers had blossomed in tandem. Anya, having secured a coveted research grant, was on the cusp of a breakthrough project that bridged the gap between art and science. Kai, his artistic reputation solidified by critically acclaimed exhibitions, had become a sought-after artist, his work displayed in galleries across the globe.

However, the relentless pursuit of professional success had begun to cast a shadow on their personal lives. Anya, consumed by the pressure to publish groundbreaking research, found herself working long hours in the lab, leaving little time for shared moments with Kai. Kai, grappling with the demands of international exhibitions and tight deadlines, felt his creative spark dimming under the pressure.

The comfortable routines they had established began to fray. Shared breakfasts became rushed affairs, stolen moments between Anya's hurried exits and Kai's late-night arrivals. Weekends, once dedicated to exploring hidden corners of the city or simply enjoying each other's company, were increasingly filled with work commitments.

One particularly tense evening, as Anya slumped onto the couch, exhaustion etched on her face, a familiar emptiness settled upon her. Glancing across the room, she saw Kai hunched over his laptop, his brow furrowed in concentration. The vibrant energy that had once filled their apartment seemed to have dimmed, replaced by a sense of quiet desperation.

"Kai," Anya began hesitantly, her voice barely above a whisper.

Kai, startled from his work, looked up, his eyes reflecting the same exhaustion that mirrored her own. "Yes, Anya?" he replied, his voice devoid of its usual warmth.

Anya took a deep breath, her heart heavy with unspoken emotions. "Do you ever feel like... we've lost sight of each other?"

Kai's gaze dropped back to his laptop screen, a tense silence engulfing the room. Finally, he sighed, a weary acceptance lacing his voice. "Maybe a little," he admitted. "Work has taken over, haven't it?"

Anya offered a small, sad smile. "It has, hasn't it?"

They sat in silence for a while, the unspoken weight of their neglect hanging heavy in the air. Anya knew something needed to change. Their love story, once a vibrant masterpiece, was in danger of fading unless they rekindled the spark that had brought them together.

• • ❧ • •

THE CONVERSATION THAT night marked a turning point. Anya and Kai, their vulnerability laid bare, embarked on a journey of rediscovery. They dusted off the self-help book they had purchased years ago, its once-familiar pages now holding a new meaning. Revisited passages offered forgotten tools – the importance of open communication, quality time, and celebrating each other's triumphs.

Taking the first step, they cleared their schedules, carving out dedicated time for each other, a weekly "date night" devoid of work discussions and distractions. They rediscovered the joy of simple pleasures – exploring new coffee shops, taking long walks hand-in-hand, and sharing childhood stories under the starlit sky.

Their conversations, once focused on career aspirations and deadlines, shifted towards a deeper understanding. Anya opened up about the pressure she felt to constantly achieve, the fear of failure gnawing at her creativity. Kai confessed his anxieties about staying relevant in the fast-paced art world, the constant need to outdo himself threatening to stifle his artistic voice.

Their support for each other became their anchor. Anya, understanding Kai's struggles, volunteered to manage his exhibition schedules, freeing him from the administrative burden. Kai, in turn, became Anya's sounding board, encouraging her to take creative risks in her research, reminding her of the intrinsic joy that fueled her passion in the first place.

They also learned to incorporate their individual passions into their shared life. Anya, inspired by Kai's artistic vision, started a personal art project, sketching intricate cellular structures with an artist's eye, capturing their beauty and complexity. Kai, intrigued by Anya's research, started incorporating scientific themes into his artwork in new and innovative ways.

Their apartment, once a neglected space, became a vibrant hub of creativity once again. Anya's meticulously detailed sketches adorned the walls alongside Kai's abstract portrayals of scientific phenomena. Late nights were no longer fueled by anxieties but by shared inspiration, their conversations a blend of scientific discoveries and artistic interpretations.

The change wasn't always easy. There were days when work pressures threatened to consume them, old anxieties rearing their heads. But through it all, they held onto their newfound commitment to each other. They learned to communicate openly, recognizing the warning signs of neglect, and proactively making time for their relationship.

The rediscovery of their love story wasn't a return to the past, but an evolution. They were no longer the naive young lovers they once were, but a seasoned couple, their love story richer and deeper, woven with the threads of shared experiences, mutual respect, and unwavering support.

One evening, as they sat on their balcony, the city lights twinkling below, reminiscing about their journey, a sense of peace settled upon them. Anya leaned into Kai's embrace, a contented sigh escaping her lips. "Remember when we first moved in here?" she mused.

Kai chuckled, a spark of his old playful spirit returning to his eyes. "How could I forget? We were so young, so full of dreams."

Anya smiled, a newfound wisdom gracing her features. "And we still are," she countered, her voice filled with conviction. "Our dreams have just evolved, just like our love story."

They gazed out at the city skyline, a symbol of their shared ambitions. Their journey together wasn't over. There would be new challenges, new chapters to be written. But they faced the future hand in hand, their love story a testament to the enduring power of connection, a vibrant masterpiece constantly evolving, forever a work in progress, painted with the colors of their ever-growing love.

Anya's research project, a culmination of years of dedication and fueled by their renewed creative synergy, culminated in a groundbreaking exhibit titled "The Symphony of Science." It showcased her research findings brought to life through stunning visuals, a captivating blend of scientific accuracy and artistic expression. Kai, a key collaborator on the project, created captivating installations that translated complex scientific concepts into a language accessible to a wider audience.

The exhibit became a resounding success, drawing crowds from all walks of life. Scientists marveled at the artistic interpretation, while art enthusiasts found themselves captivated by the scientific insights woven into the visuals. Anya and Kai, basking in the positive reception, felt a surge of pride. It was a testament to their combined talents, a symbol of their love story taking center stage, inspiring and educating others.

The success of the exhibit opened new doors for them. Anya received invitations to speak at prestigious conferences, sharing her research and its artistic interpretation. Kai, his artistic reputation further solidified by the collaborative work, found himself collaborating with museums and science institutions, his artwork now bridging the gap between the scientific and artistic communities.

However, their newfound fame brought with it its own set of challenges. The increased time demands pulled them in different directions. Anya found herself traveling extensively for conferences, while Kai's international exhibitions kept him away from home for weeks on end. The comfortable routine they had painstakingly re-established threatened to unravel once again.

One evening, after a particularly long separation, Anya returned home to an empty apartment, a familiar sense of loneliness washing over her. Kai, caught up in a last-minute exhibition setup in a different country, could only offer apologies and promises over a video call. Anya, the loneliness gnawing at her, found herself questioning their future.

The following days were strained. Communication, once their strongest suit, became fractured, filled with unspoken resentments. Finally, unable to bear the emotional distance any longer, Anya sat Kai down for a heart-to-heart conversation.

"We can't keep doing this, Kai," she confessed, her voice trembling slightly. "Our careers are taking us in different directions, and our relationship is suffering."

Kai, his face etched with concern, mirrored her emotions. "I know, Anya," he admitted. "But what are we supposed to do? Give up everything we've worked so hard for?"

Anya took a deep breath, her eyes searching his. "No, of course not," she replied. "But maybe we need to find a way to balance it all. Maybe we don't have to be apart all the time."

The following weeks were filled with brainstorming sessions. They explored possibilities, their love for each other a constant guiding light. Finally, a solution emerged – a compromise fueled by creativity. Anya, inspired by their long-distance video calls, proposed a live-streamed art project. They would use their travels as inspiration, creating collaborative artwork remotely, sharing the process with a global audience.

Kai, his eyes sparkling with newfound excitement, readily agreed. "It's perfect, Anya," he exclaimed. "We get to share our passions with the world, and we stay connected, no matter where we are."

Their project, aptly titled "Love Across Latitudes," became an instant sensation. People from all corners of the globe tuned in to watch their creative process unfold, captivated by the artistry and the underlying love story. Anya, from a bustling conference venue in Japan, would describe a scientific concept. Kai, from his studio in a bustling European city, would translate it into a captivating visual, their collaboration a testament to their enduring connection.

The project wasn't just artistic; it was a symbol of their commitment to each other. They had learned to navigate the challenges of a life intertwined with ambition and distance. Their love story, once a fragile seedling, had blossomed into a vibrant tapestry, woven with the threads of compromise, creative collaboration, and an unwavering belief in the power of their connection. They were living proof that love, like art, could transcend boundaries, forever a work in progress, forever evolving, a masterpiece painted on the grand canvas of life.

Years rolled by, each brushstroke on the canvas of their lives adding a new layer of experience and depth to their love story. Their live-streamed art project, "Love Across Latitudes," continued to evolve, becoming a global phenomenon. Anya, a renowned scientist at the forefront of science communication, captivated audiences with her engaging explanations. Kai, a celebrated artist known for his innovative blend of science and art, translated her words into stunning visuals.

Their travels took them to every corner of the globe, from the bustling streets of Tokyo to the serene beauty of the Amazon rainforest. Each new environment served as inspiration, their collaboration adapting to the unique cultural landscapes they encountered. Anya's scientific discoveries were influenced by ancient traditions, while Kai's artwork resonated with the stories and struggles of the people they met.

However, amidst the whirlwind of success, the yearning for a permanent home began to simmer within them. Anya, exhausted from the constant jet lag, craved a place to unwind, a refuge to nurture her creativity. Kai, longing for a dedicated studio space where he wouldn't have to constantly dismantle and rebuild his artistic sanctuary, yearned for a sense of stability.

One evening, during a particularly grueling project deadline met over a shaky video call, they made a spontaneous decision. "Let's find a home, Kai," Anya declared, the weariness in her voice laced with a newfound determination.

Kai, a weary smile gracing his features, echoed her sentiment. "A place where we can create, a place where we can grow old together."

The search for their permanent home wasn't easy. They envisioned a haven that could accommodate their individual needs, a space that would inspire and nurture their creativity. It had to be a place that resonated with their shared love for exploration, yet offered a sense of stability.

Finally, tucked away in a charming coastal town, they stumbled upon a quaint, two-story house with a spacious attic and a sprawling backyard overlooking the ocean. It was as if the house itself had been waiting for them, its creaky floorboards and sun-drenched rooms whispering stories of adventures yet to come.

Transforming the house became a collaborative project. Anya, inspired by the natural beauty surrounding them, designed an indoor greenhouse where she could cultivate plants for her scientific research. Kai, captivated by the ever-changing colors of the ocean, created a dedicated studio space in the attic, its windows framing breathtaking views of the horizon.

Their lives in this new haven settled into a comfortable rhythm. Mornings were spent side-by-side in their respective workspaces, fueled by coffee and stolen kisses. Afternoons were dedicated to shared adventures – exploring hidden coves along the coastline, their laughter echoing through the salty breeze. Evenings were filled with discussions about their latest projects, their creative energies intertwining as they shared ideas and offered each other support.

The house became more than just a physical space; it became a symbol of their enduring love. It was a testament to their journey - a long road paved with challenges, compromises, and unwavering commitment. They had learned to navigate the complexities of a life intertwined with ambition and distance, their love story a masterpiece constantly evolving.

One starlit night, as they sat on their porch, the sound of crashing waves filling the air, Anya snuggled closer to Kai, a contented sigh escaping her lips. Looking up at the vast expanse of the night sky, she whispered, "Remember when we thought long-distance was the hardest thing we'd ever face?"

Kai chuckled, his arm wrapping around her shoulders. "Who knew life would throw so many more challenges our way?"

Anya smiled, her eyes sparkling with affection. "But we faced them together, didn't we? And somehow, our love story only grew stronger."

They sat in comfortable silence, the rhythmic sound of the ocean a soothing soundtrack to their shared memories. Their journey wasn't over. There would be new obstacles, new chapters to be written. But as they gazed out at the endless horizon, hand in hand, they knew they would face them together, their love story a vibrant masterpiece forever in progress, forever a testament to the enduring power of connection, a love story painted on the grand canvas of life, with every sunrise a new brushstroke waiting to be made.

Conclusion:

Anya and Kai's journey, a tapestry woven with the threads of love, art, and science, culminated in a symphony of shared experiences, unwavering support, and an enduring connection that transcended boundaries. Their love story, painted on the grand canvas of life, was a testament to the power of human connection, a reminder that even amidst the challenges and uncertainties of life, love could persevere, evolving and deepening with each passing chapter.

. . ❧ . .

THE ART OF COLLABORATION:

From their first tentative steps into cohabitation to their global artistic collaborations, Anya and Kai's relationship was a testament to the power of teamwork. They recognized each other's strengths and weaknesses, leveraging their individual talents to create a synergy that far surpassed the sum of its parts.

Anya's scientific rigor and Kai's artistic flair complemented each other beautifully. Anya's ability to dissect complex concepts and translate them into accessible language inspired Kai's artistic interpretations, while Kai's ability to capture the essence of scientific ideas through his art sparked Anya's creativity and broadened her perspective.

Their collaborative projects, from the live-streamed art project "Love Across Latitudes" to their shared scientific research, became a testament to their ability to bridge the gap between seemingly disparate disciplines. They demonstrated that art and science were not mutually exclusive but rather complementary forces, each enriching the other and offering unique insights into the world around them.

Navigating the Challenges of Distance

The demands of their respective careers often pulled Anya and Kai in different directions, testing the resilience of their love story. They faced the challenges of long-distance relationships, grappling with the loneliness and uncertainty that came with being apart for extended periods.

However, amidst the challenges, they discovered new ways to connect and nurture their bond. They embraced technology, using video calls and social media to stay in touch and share their daily experiences. They found creative ways to collaborate remotely, turning their physical distance into an opportunity to explore new artistic expressions and deepen their understanding of each other.

Their ability to adapt and find innovative solutions to the challenges of distance demonstrated the strength of their connection. They learned to trust each other, to communicate openly and honestly, and to prioritize their relationship despite the demands of their careers.

• • ⌘ • •

THE EVOLVING TAPESTRY of Love:

Anya and Kai's love story was not a static entity but a dynamic tapestry that evolved with time and experience. They grew as individuals, their passions and perspectives shaping their relationship in new and unexpected ways.

Anya's scientific research took her to the forefront of science communication, while Kai's artistic reputation soared as he gained international acclaim. Their individual successes brought them new opportunities and challenges, but their love story remained their anchor, a source of support and inspiration.

They embraced the changes, recognizing that their love story was not about remaining the same but about growing together. They learned to celebrate each other's achievements, to offer support during setbacks, and to encourage each other to pursue their dreams.

Anya and Kai's love story was a testament to the enduring power of human connection. It was a story of two individuals who found each other, navigated the challenges of life together, and emerged stronger and more connected. Their love story was a reminder that love could transcend boundaries, evolve with time, and serve as a source of strength and inspiration amidst the uncertainties of life.

Their journey, a symphony of love, art, and science, continued to unfold, each new chapter painted with the vibrant colors of their shared experiences and unwavering commitment to each other. Their love story was a masterpiece in progress, a testament to the enduring power of human connection, a beacon of hope in a world that often seemed uncertain and chaotic.

About the Author

Mrigendra Bharti, born on June 29, 2004, in South Delhi, India, is a multifaceted individual recognized as the owner of Mrigendra Bharti Group InfoTech India Co. Pvt Ltd. Beyond his entrepreneurial endeavors, he is a distinguished music producer, director, and a budding writer.

Embarking on his professional journey at a young age, Mrigendra Bharti's visionary leadership has led to the establishment of several successful ventures, including Croma Music Series Entertainment, Sellbrochure, Fauget Innovative, and more.

What sets Mrigendra apart is his early initiation into the world of business. His foray into the unknown realms of entrepreneurship began during his 10th-grade years, where he delved into the music industry. This initial venture laid the foundation for subsequent achievements, showcasing his dedication and resilience.

Having honed his skills in music, Mrigendra Bharti not only demonstrated significant growth in his craft but also expanded his professional network. His passion extends beyond music, encompassing app and website development, as well as graphic design.

Fueled by his creative aspirations, Mrigendra established the Mrigendra Bharti Group, a company specializing in website and app development. Currently, he collaborates with a dedicated team, collectively working on ambitious projects that promise innovation and excellence.

Mrigendra's journey serves as an inspiration, particularly for today's students, highlighting the potential of youthful determination and the ability to transform innovative ideas into successful businesses. As he continues to make strides in various domains, Mrigendra Bharti remains a dynamic force, contributing vibrancy to the realms of business, music, and technology.

Read more at https://www.imwriter-mrigendra.rf.gd.